THE LIGHT within ME

D0926107

written by
Lauren Grabois Fischer
pictures by
Devin Hunt 11.23.2020

The Be Books

www.TheBEbooks.com

Jonah
Be the Light!
Lauren

I hope that you enjoy this book and the fun activities that follow after. If you come up with a great activity that promotes kindness, positivity, and love, and you want to share it with me, you can email your ideas to **lauren@thebebooks.com** or find me on social media **@thebebooks!**

You can follow my page for positive posts, updates on book giveaways, and new books coming out. I would love to share your beautiful creations with others. You can have your parents post them on social media and tag **@thebebooks**. Make sure to use **#thebebooks**, **#beyou**, and **#bethelightbethechange** in your posts.

This book is dedicated to the light within us all. May we each be able to recognize the power that we have to make this world a brighter, more beautiful, more peaceful place.

I have always been fascinated that one lantern can light up an entire room of darkness. We must each realize that this world needs our light and our unique perspective. If we work together, we can live in a world full of love, peace and harmony.

To Isaac and Mollie... your smiles light up my world.

I have a

Light
within
Me.

When I am happy,

excited

confident

and positive
       it shines ever so brightly.

it dims so low that
I too can't see
my own
bright light.

I have the power to either leave

my light

ON

or to turn it

OFF

This light
within me,
can light
up my
Home.

It can
light up
my

Community.

It can

light up

my

State.

It can
light up
my
Country.

It can
light up
the
World.

But what is it?

Why do I have a
light within me?

Why was I given
this light?

Every single one of us
has a light within.

What will we do with it?

Will we share it?

Will we hide it?

Will we make this world
brighter or will we darken it?

Will we use our powers
for the good or for the bad?

This is our choice.
This is our power

I choose to lighten up the world.

I choose to brighten even
the darkest night.

I choose

to bring joy and laughter
and positivity to those who meet me.
I choose light.

You can too.

You too have the ability to turn a dark room into a bright room.

You too can make someone smile and make their day even brighter.

But there is more.
My light is not just for me.

My light has a magic power.
It can be shared.

The light within me
can become the light
within you!

And the coolest part is... that when I share my light,

my light only grows stronger! It never dims!

TOGETHER,

We can light up even
more of the world.

TOGETHER,
Our light can electrify and empower the world.

We can continue to spread the light to others and slowly.... the world will become a more beautiful, more positive, more happy, more loving, more accepting,

more brilliant,
more illuminated place!

Inspiration & Discussion

• What are some ways that you can make this world a brighter place? Talk with your parents, siblings and friends about things that you can do to add more light into our world.

• Make it a goal of yours today to make at least five people smile. There are lots of fun and creative ways to do that. Hold a door open for someone. Tell someone a joke. Hug your parents. Tell those that you love just how much you love them. Share a toy with a friend. Help someone with their homework. Can you think of ways to make someone smile?

• Donating old toys and old clothes is a great way to give back to your community. Tell your parents that you would love to donate things that you do not use in your home. You can find a location that you can drop off your donations. Knowing that you are helping someone else will not only make someone else happy, but you yourself will feel brighter too.

- Be grateful. Every day when you wake up in the morning, think of five to ten things that you love about your life. You can make this a fun family activity. Everyone can say what they are thankful for. Thinking of positive things can brighten your day and make you smile.

- What is something that you love to do? Make sure that you fill your days with people and things that you love. Every single day is a gift and we should be thankful for it.

- Use your light for the good. Be positive. Be confident. Listen to your heart and be true to yourself. Your energy can help heal the world or it can hurt the world. Make sure that you are being kind and loving and accepting to all. Be the change. Be the light.

- Bring your positivity into your school/workplace. Greet others with a friendly smile and a warm hug or handshake. Be someones reason to smile and laugh.

Activity Pages

"The Light Within Me" will hopefully inspire you to share your light with the world. It is important that we take care of our light and ourselves. Being mindful is a great way to develop those skills. Taking the time to enjoy the moment that you are in is so important.

• **Meditating:** A wonderful activity to do with your family or by yourself is to sit quietly and listen to your breath. Find a comfortable spot in your house and sit down. Close your eyes and breathe and relax. You can count your breathing like this: "In, 2, 3, Out, 2, 3, In, 2, 3, Out, 2, 3, In, 2, 3, Out, 2, 3". Aim to sit for a minute the first time. You can practice for one minute a day for one week. Increase it to two minutes when you feel ready. And then feel free to increase the time as you desire. A good idea is to increase the amount of minutes to the number of your age. If you are four, you can sit for up to four minutes. If you are six, you can sit for up to six minutes. Ten to twenty minutes is a good amount of time to meditate daily. You will be so grateful to yourself for taking the time to relax and enjoy your breath and some quiet time.

• **Mirror Work:** Stand in front of your mirror and look at yourself in the eyes. Use "I am" and "I can" statements that are kind and loving. You are very special and you should compliment yourself for the great job that you are doing. Below are some sample sentences that you can speak kindly to yourself. "I am happy. I am healthy. I am brave. I am responsible. I am strong. I am loved. I am confident. I am beautiful inside and out. I can do anything. I am safe." Practice this every day and you will see that the positivity and happiness will fill your heart.

• **Gratitude List:** Use the lines below to write five things that you are grateful for.

1. _____

2. _____

3. _____

4. _____

5. _____

• **Stretching/Exercising:** Our bodies do so much for us. Take the time to say thank you to your body. Go on a daily walk. Go outside and kick a ball with your family. Run and play in the sun. Get out of the house and break a sweat. And after you are all done having fun, find time to stretch your legs and stretch your arms. There are so many wonderful ways to stretch your bodies. Ask your parents to find a great plan for you. Yoga is a wonderful way to say thank you to our bodies.

I am thankful for each of you! Thank you for taking the time to read this book and to reflect on your purpose in this world! Each time that you read "The Light Within Me", I hope that it inspires you to smile, laugh, love and be yourself! After all, there is only one you! You can make this world a brighter, more kind, more respectful, more accepting, more beautiful place!

Let your inner light shine so brightly that the world will reflect your positivity everywhere.

I honor the light within you.

Namaste.

With love and gratitude,

Lauren Grabois Fischer